Snore!

For Tom and Oliver
and Daniel the Artist
JL

First published in hardback in Great Britain by HarperCollins Publishers Ltd in 1998
First published in paperback by Picture Lions in 1999
This edition published by Collins Picture Books in 2003
3 5 7 9 10 8 6 4 2 1
ISBN: 0 00 773586 3
Picture Lions and Collins Picture Books are imprints of the Children's Division,
part of HarperCollins Publishers Ltd.
Text copyright © Michael Rosen 1998
Illustrations copyright © Jonathan Langley 1998
Cover illustration copyright © Jonathan Langley 2003
The author and illustrator assert the moral right to be identified as the author and illustrator of the work.
A CIP catalogue record for this title is available from the British Library.
Visit our website at: www.harpercollinschildrensbooks.co.uk
Printed in Italy

HarperCollins Children's Books supports Bookstart.

Snore!

Michael Rosen

illustrated by Jonathan Langley

HarperCollins Children's Books

All was quiet on the farm.

Dog was asleep.   Cat was asleep.

Cow was asleep.

Sheep was asleep.

Pig was asleep,

and so were all the Piglets.

It was all so peaceful – till...

snore!

and Cat woke up.

Cow woke up.

Sheep woke up.

Pig woke up, and so did all the Piglets.

It was so loud no one could sleep,
not Cat, or Cow, or Sheep, or Pig,
nor all the Piglets.

snore!

How can we get Dog to stop snoring
so we can all get back to sleep?
said Cat.

I know, said Cow – and Cow
went up to Dog and went
ATTISSHOOO
right down his ear.

snore!

I know, said Sheep – and Sheep
went up to Dog and
went **BOO** right
down his ear.

snore!

I know, said Pig – and Pig went up to
Dog and went **HEE HEE**
right down his ear, and
all the Piglets went
HEE HEE HEE HEE.

snore!

I know, said Cat, why don't we
sing to him?

Maybe that'll stop him snoring and
we can all go back to sleep.

So Cat went **PURRRR.**

snore!

And Cow went **MOOO.**

snore!

And Sheep went **BAAA.**

snore!

And Pig went **OINK** and all the Piglets went **GRUNT GRUNT GRUNT GRUNT.**

snore!

Then as the sun rose over the trees,
Rooster woke up with a
**COCK-A-DOODLE-
DOOOOO,**

and Dog woke
up with a
HERUMPH???

And off he trotted down the
road after his good night's sleep.

But Cat and Cow and Sheep and
Pig and all the Piglets were so tired...
they fell asleep.

snore!

snore!

Michael Rosen & Jonathan Langley

Oww!

A wriggly piglet with a prickly problem

ISBN: 0-00-712442-2 HB
ISBN: 0-00-712443-0 PB

Piggy Piglet sits on something very prickly – and he can't get it off! Can any of his friends in the farmyard help him?

Another warm, funny story from Michael Rosen about Pig and her Piglets, Dog, Cat, Sheep, Cow and not forgetting grumpy Donkey…

ISBN: 0-00-664698-0 PB

ISBN: 0-00-711538-5 HB
ISBN: 0-00-711539-3 PB

ISBN: 0-00-664681-6 PB

Jonathan Langley's picture books are favourites for very young children. *Snore!* was chosen by The Guardian as one of the best children's books of the year and it was 1998 Gold Award Winner in the Best Illustrated Book category in Parents Magazine 'Play and Learn Awards'.